THE LOST CHILDREN

THE LOST CHILDREN
the boys who were neglected

story and illustrations by
PAUL GOBLE

Aladdin Paperbacks

First Aladdin Paperbacks edition June 1998
Copyright © 1993 by Paul Goble

Aladdin Paperbacks
An imprint of Simon & Schuster Children's Publishing Division
1230 Avenue of the Americas
New York, NY 10020

Also available in a Simon & Schuster
Books for Young Readers hardcover edition.
Designed by Paul Goble
Printed in Hong Kong
10 9 8 7 6 5 4 3

The Library of Congress has cataloged the hardcover edition
as follows:
Goble, Paul
The lost children: the boys who were neglected / story and
illustrations by Paul Goble. —
1st ed.
p.   cm.
Summary: A Blackfoot Indian legend in which six neglected
orphaned brothers decide to go to the Above World where they
become the constellation of the "Lost Children," or Pleiades.

ISBN 0-02-736555-7
1. Siksika Indians—Legends. 2. Stars—Folklore.
[1. Siksika Indians—Legends. 2.
Indians of North America—Legends. 3. Stars—Folklore.]
I. Title
E99.S54G62   1993
398.21'0899736—dc20
91-44283
[E]

ISBN 0-689-81999-4 (pbk.)

REFERENCES: Ella C. Clark, *Indian Legends from the
Northern Rockies*, University of Oklahoma Press, Norman,
1966; George B. Grinnell, *Blackfoot Lodge Tales*, Charles
Scribner's Sons, New York, 1892; Adolph Hungry Wolf, *The
Blood People; A Division of the Blackfoot Confederacy*, Harper
and Row, New York, 1977; *Painted Tipis by Contemporary
Plains Indian Artists*, Indian Arts and Crafts Board of the US
Department of the Interior, Anadarko, 1973; Robert Lowie,
Myths and Traditions of the Crow Indians, Anthropological
Papers of the American Museum of Natural History, Vol
XXV, New York, 1918; Museum of the Rockies, *Blackfoot
Tipis: Design and Legend*, Bozeman, 1976; Walter McClintock,
*The Old North Trail; Life, Legends and Religion of the Blackfeet
Indians*, Macmillan, London, 1910; Stith Thompson, *Tales of
the North American Indians*, Indiana University Press,
Bloomington, 1929; Robert N. Wilson, "Blackfoot Star
Myths: The Pleiades," *The American Antiquarian and Oriental
Journal*, No 15, 1893; Clark Wissler, *Star Legends Among the
American Indians*, American Museum of Natural History
Guide Leaflet Series, No 91, New York, 1936; Clark Wissler
and D. C. Duvall, *Blackfoot Mythology*, Anthropological
Papers of the American Museum of Natural History, Vol II,
New York, 1908.

for my son, Robert, with all my love

AUTHOR'S NOTE:

This story is based on a sacred Blackfoot myth, telling the origin of the Pleiades stars, which they call the Bunched Stars or *the Lost Children*. Indian people from most of North America tell a similar story: the Pleiades were once children who went to the Sky World because people did not look after them. It is a sad and shocking, and also quite sentimental story. This retelling follows the tone of the oldest versions recorded between 1890 and 1920 (see References), where the language used is straightforward, without descriptions, in order that listeners can imagine the story for themselves.

It is sometimes imagined that these myths have been handed down, word-for-word, since time immemorial. Only the themes, the ideas, were passed down, and storytellers wove around them. A hundred years ago a Blackfoot storyteller explained it by pulling up a weed: "The parts of this weed all branch from the stem. They go different ways, but all come from the same root. So it is with the different versions of a myth." It should be understood that these myths were never simply fanciful tales; they contain the essential truths, like the Scriptures.

Blackfoot painted tipis have the Bunched Stars, *the Lost Children*, painted on the south smoke flap; a visible reminder of this story and of the need to look after all the little children. Variants of the Bunched Stars, as painted on Blackfoot tipis, are shown on this page. For more explanations of tipi designs, see page 32.

On the Great Plains the sky is immense, and in the dry air the stars appear bright and close. No wonder that the Blackfoot have wonderful stories about the stars and life in the Above World. Looking up through the smoke hole of the tipi, you see the stars forever turning around the Star that Stands Still, the Pole Star, like dancers moving around the dance circle. You feel these ancient stories come alive.

*T*his is a story about the
world which is above our
world. In the old days it was
told after dark. If we close our
eyes we can go back to those
days. . . .
We are sitting on buffalo robes
in the tipi. The fire at the
center casts our flickering
shadows on the painted lining
behind us. Someone takes a
red-hot coal from the fire with
wooden tongs, and places it
on the ground in front of the
storyteller. A little dry sweet-
grass is dropped on it, filling
the lodge with a sweet smell,
which pleases the good spirits.

The storyteller slowly washes her hands in the smoke, and then passes them over her head and body to purify herself. She is ready to begin.... The Star People are looking down at us through the smoke hole, and will hear the truth of what she says:—

Children are given to us by the Great Spirit. Yes, they are God's greatest gifts. And yet, sometimes we forget, and we are not kind to them. This is a story about what happened when the people did not look after six little children.

A long time ago there were six children who were brothers. Their mother and father were dead. They had no home, and no family to look after them. They slept and ate in one place today, and another tomorrow, and they were always hungry. Their only clothes were what people had discarded.

Although the children had no family, the camp dogs loved them, and they loved the dogs. They played and wandered around happily together all day long. They helped to look after each other in many ways, and when night came they often shared the same bed.

Nobody was kind to the brothers. Nobody wanted them. Other children chased them, and threw stones, and laughed at their ragged clothes and tangled hair.

Each year it was the custom
for families to honor their
children by giving them
little yellow calf robes after
the early summer buffalo
hunt. But nobody gave new
robes to the brothers. The
other children flaunted
their new robes and fine
clothes, and teased the
brothers in their ragged
clothes.
"Shabby old bulls!" they
called them.

The children were sad.
They wanted to find
another home. They did
not even wish to be people
any longer. And so they
argued among themselves
about what they should be.
"Let's be flowers."
"No, the buffaloes will eat
us."
"Then let's be stones."
"Stones break into small
stones."
"Well, let's be water."
"No, animals and people
will drink us."

"Let's be trees."
"Trees are cut down for
firewood."
In the end they agreed to be
stars.
"Stars remain forever. We
will always be beautiful.
People will watch us, and
they will know when the
seasons are changing."

One of the children led the
way to the sky.
"Shut your eyes! Do not
look back!" he warned. He
blew a feather into the air,
and they were lifted toward
the Above World.
One of them did look back.
He is now Smoking Star,
the comet.

When the children opened their eyes they were standing on a beautiful prairie in front of Sun Man's tipi. They entered the tipi, and the inside was as big as the sky. Sun Man was at home with Moon Woman, his wife. He asked the children why they had come.

"People were unkind to us," they answered. "Nobody gave us new yellow calf robes. We only have old clothes. We want to live where people will be kind to us. We want to live here."

Moon Woman wept and clasped them in her arms. "My poor lost children," she called them.

Sun Man was angry. "I will punish the people who have not looked after these little children," he said, and he shone down on the earth with terrible heat. The grass died, forests burned, and ponds dried up. The earth cracked open and hot winds blew clouds of dust. People, and every bird and animal as well, suffered dreadful thirst.

One morning, before the
sun rose, the dogs began to
howl. First one, and then
all, looked up into the sky
and howled, and even the
wolves and coyotes joined
them.
The wise men told the people: "The dogs are sad and
lonely because their friends,
the lost children, have gone
to the Above World. They
are telling us: 'You never
looked after them. You only
gave them what you did not
want. Now they're stars.'"

The old leader of the dogs
looked up and prayed:

"Listen to me! Have pity on my Dog People....
They are hot and thirsty. Everyone cries with thirst: the buffaloes walk all day long searching for grass; the butterflies are looking for flowers, and the birds are flying away because there is nothing for them to eat. We are dying. We want to live! Give us rain!"

Sun Man looked down and saw how the birds and animals suffered. He was sorry; he had only meant to punish the people because they had not been kind to the children.

He covered the sky with dark thunderclouds. Swift-flying swallows darted with the lightning and brought the rain. New life came once again to the thirsty earth.

You can see the Lost Children in the Above World. We call them the Pleiades, or the Bunched Stars, because they are close together, just as they always were when they were on earth. How beautiful the children look! And yet, how very far away they are now. If only

people had remembered that all the little children are gifts from God....
You can see many small stars close to the Lost Children.

Astronomers say they have seen more than four hundred!
Those are the camp dogs who found their friends, the children, again at last.

A NOTE ABOUT THE TIPIS:

The tipis (*niitoyis*) illustrated are from the Blackfoot nation. Most are copied from photographs taken by the author over the last twenty years in Montana and Alberta. It will be seen that in general each has a colored top, bottom border, and animal designs in between.

The bottom border is the earth with jagged mountains, rounded hills, or level plains, and with discs for "dusty stars," or puff-balls which mysteriously appear overnight, and so are related to the stars.

The top of the tipi is the Above World: a Maltese cross at the back is Morning Star, the son of Sun and Moon. On the north smoke flap (tipis face east) is a line of seven discs for the Seven Brothers, the Big Dipper. On the south flap is the group of *the Lost Children*.

It was the birds and animals who gave their tipis to man in visions, and it is they who are painted on the middle of the lodge. Picked out in different colors are the internal and external parts which contain the animal's sacred power.

Every illustrated tipi is painted, but in a camp only about ten percent are painted. The designs are ancient and have been handed down. Today there are no visions because people think more about material than spiritual things.